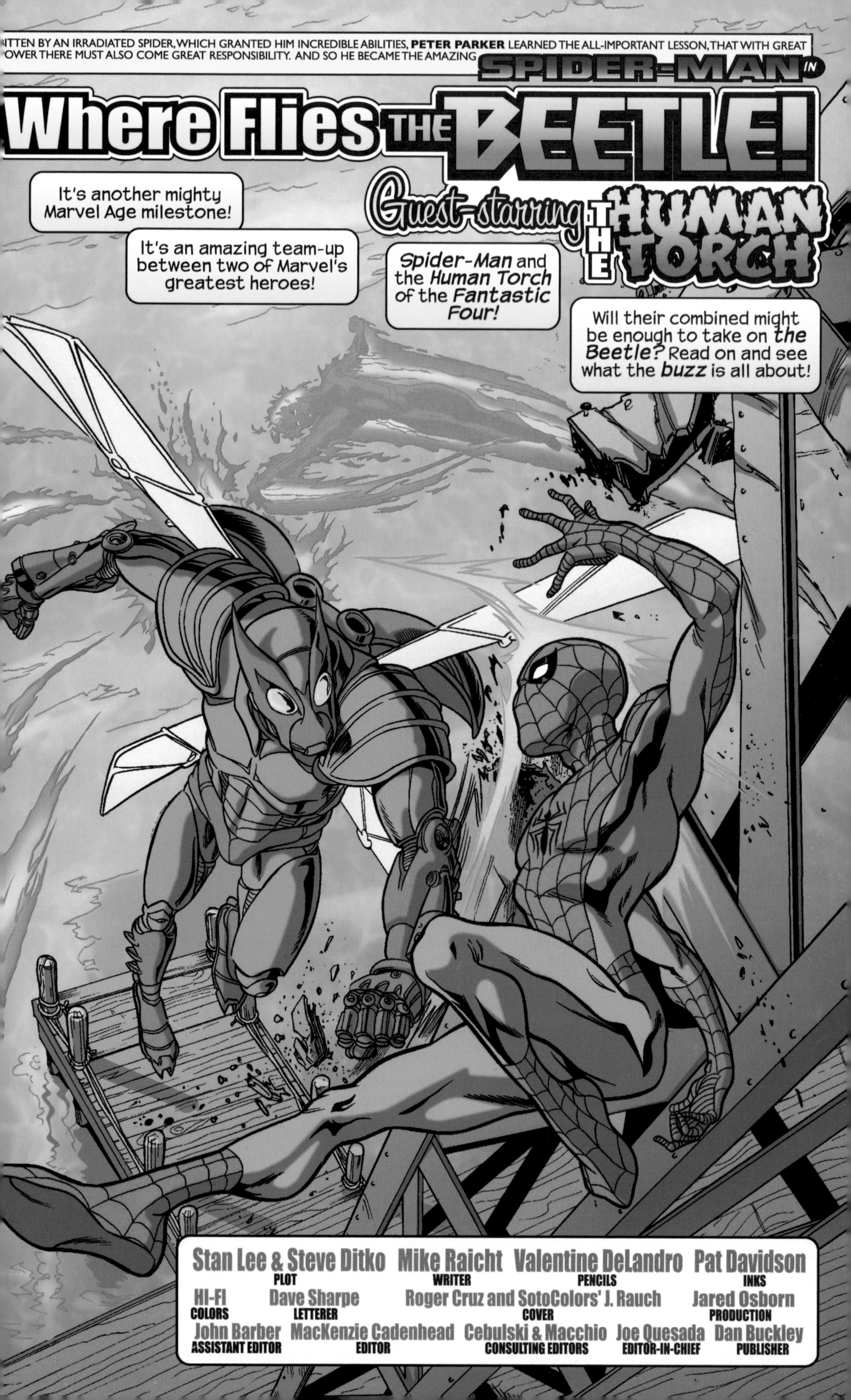

ITTEN BY AN IRRADIATED SPIDER, WHICH GRANTED HIM INCREDIBLE ABILITIES, PETER PARKER LEARNED THE ALL-IMPORTANT LESSON, THAT WITH GREAT OWER THERE MUST ALSO COME GREAT RESPONSIBILITY. AND SO HE BECAME THE AMAZING SPIDER-MAN IN
Where Flies THE BEETLE!
Guest-starring THE HUMAN TORCH
It's another mighty Marvel Age milestone!
It's an amazing team-up between two of Marvel's greatest heroes!
Spider-Man and the Human Torch of the Fantastic Four!
Will their combined might be enough to take on the Beetle? Read on and see what the buzz is all about!
Stan Lee & Steve Ditko PLOT
Mike Raicht WRITER
Valentine DeLandro PENCILS
Pat Davidson INKS
HI-FI COLORS
Dave Sharpe LETTERER
Roger Cruz and SotoColors' J. Rauch COVER
Jared Osborn PRODUCTION
John Barber ASSISTANT EDITOR
MacKenzie Cadenhead EDITOR
Cebulski & Macchio CONSULTING EDITORS
Joe Quesada EDITOR-IN-CHIEF
Dan Buckley PUBLISHER

VISIT US AT
www.abdopub.com

Spotlight, a division of ABDO Publishing Company Inc., is the school and library distributor of the Marvel Entertainment books.

Library bound edition © 2006

Library of Congress Cataloging-in-Publication Data

Where Flies the Beetle!

ISBN 1-59961-023-X   (Reinforced Library Bound Edition)

All Spotlight books are reinforced library binding and manufactured in the United States of America

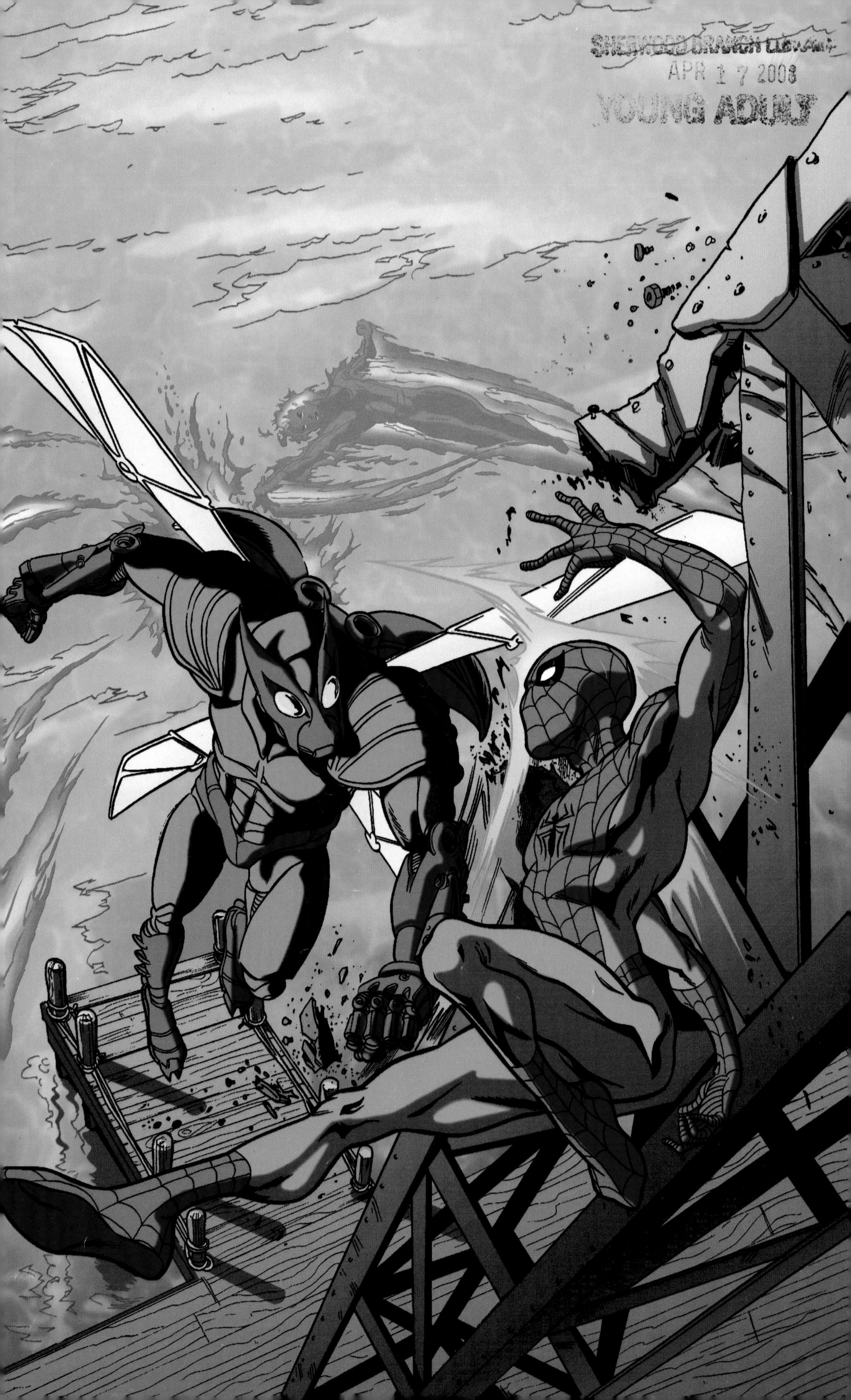

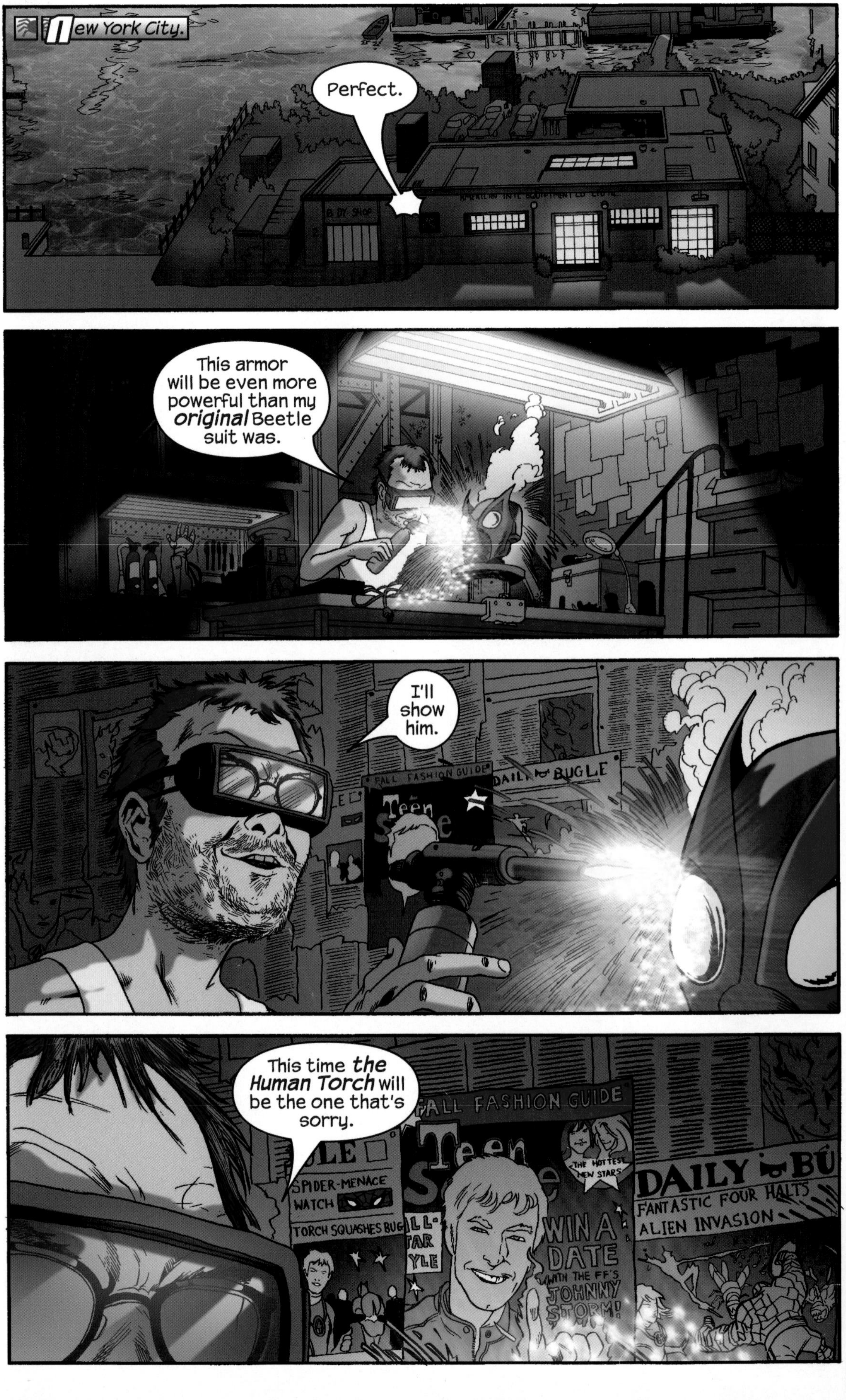
New York City.
Perfect.
This armor will be even more powerful than my *original* Beetle suit was.
I'll show him.
This time *the Human Torch* will be the one that's sorry.
SPIDER-MENACE WATCH
TORCH SQUASHES BUG
FALL FASHION GUIDE
THE HOTTEST NEW STARS
WIN A DATE WITH THE FF'S JOHNNY STORM!
FANTASTIC FOUR HALTS ALIEN INVASION

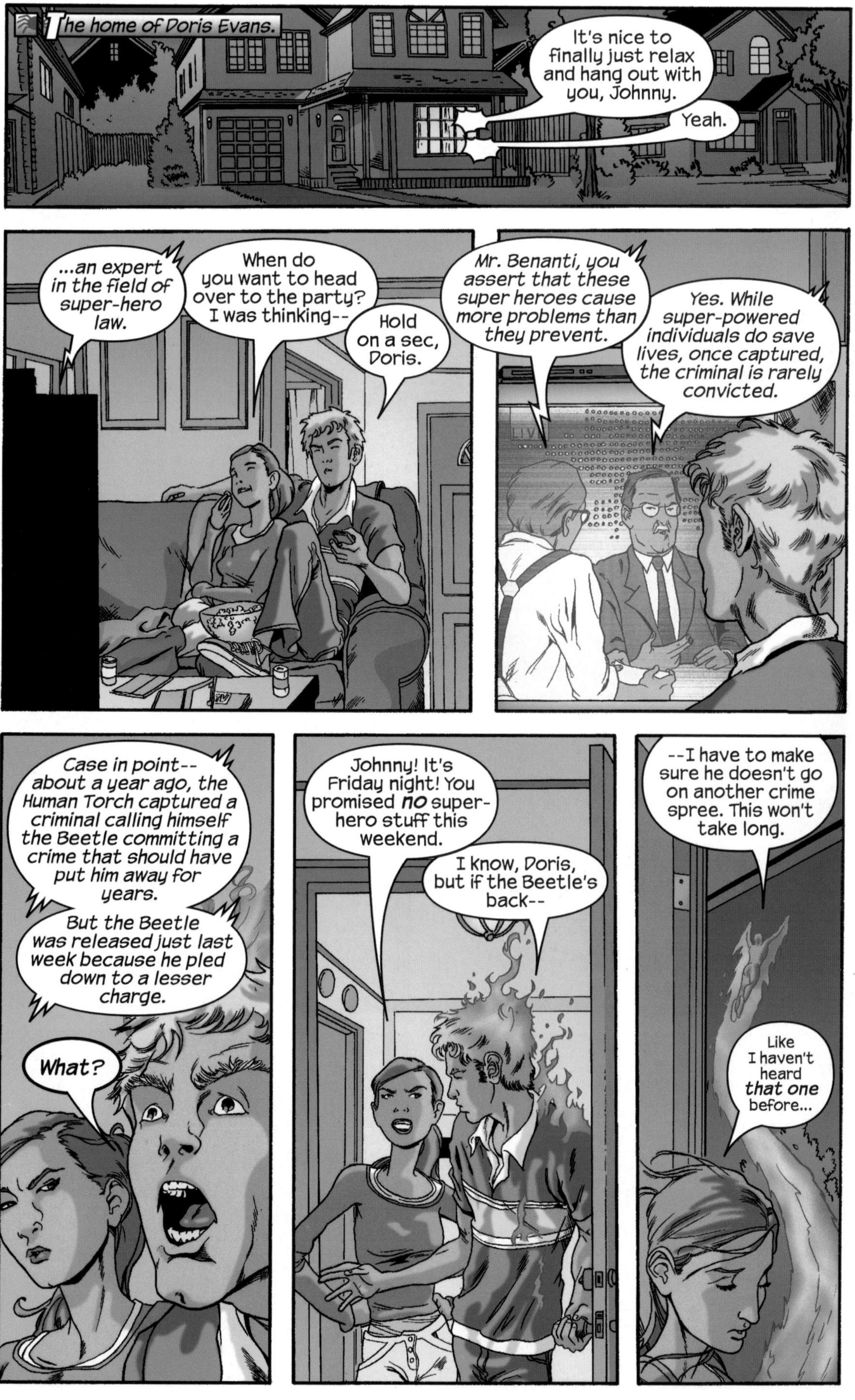

The home of Doris Evans.
It's nice to finally just relax and hang out with you, Johnny.
Yeah.
...an expert in the field of super-hero law.
When do you want to head over to the party? I was thinking--
Hold on a sec, Doris.
Mr. Benanti, you assert that these super heroes cause more problems than they prevent.
Yes. While super-powered individuals do save lives, once captured, the criminal is rarely convicted.
Case in point--about a year ago, the Human Torch captured a criminal calling himself the Beetle committing a crime that should have put him away for years.
But the Beetle was released just last week because he pled down to a lesser charge.
What?
Johnny! It's Friday night! You promised no super-hero stuff this weekend.
I know, Doris, but if the Beetle's back--
--I have to make sure he doesn't go on another crime spree. This won't take long.
Like I haven't heard that one before...

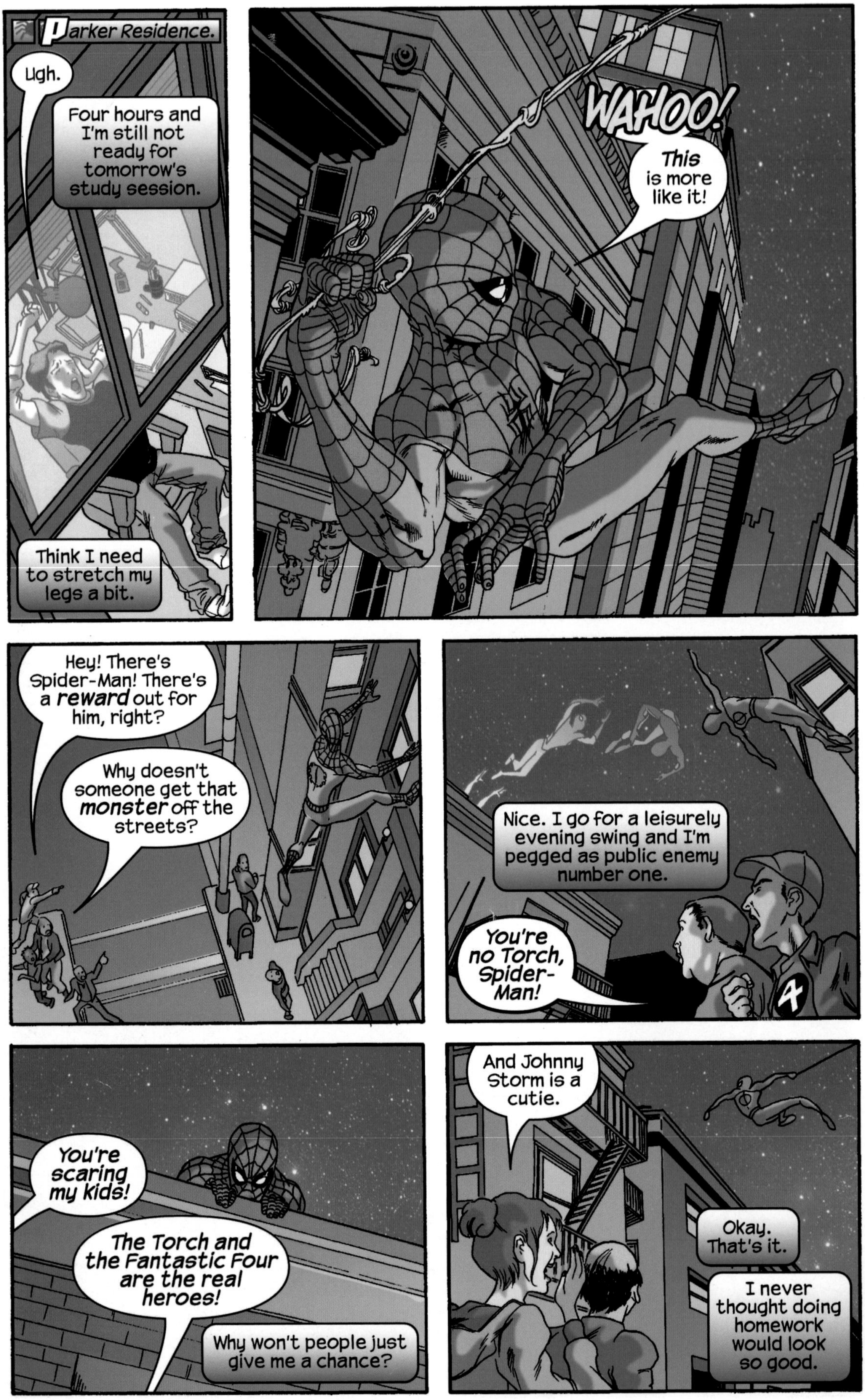

Parker Residence.
Ugh.
Four hours and I'm still not ready for tomorrow's study session.
Think I need to stretch my legs a bit.
WAHOO!
This is more like it!
Hey! There's Spider-Man! There's a reward out for him, right?
Why doesn't someone get that monster off the streets?
Nice. I go for a leisurely evening swing and I'm pegged as public enemy number one.
You're no Torch, Spider-Man!
You're scaring my kids!
The Torch and the Fantastic Four are the real heroes!
Why won't people just give me a chance?
And Johnny Storm is a cutie.
Okay. That's it.
I never thought doing homework would look so good.

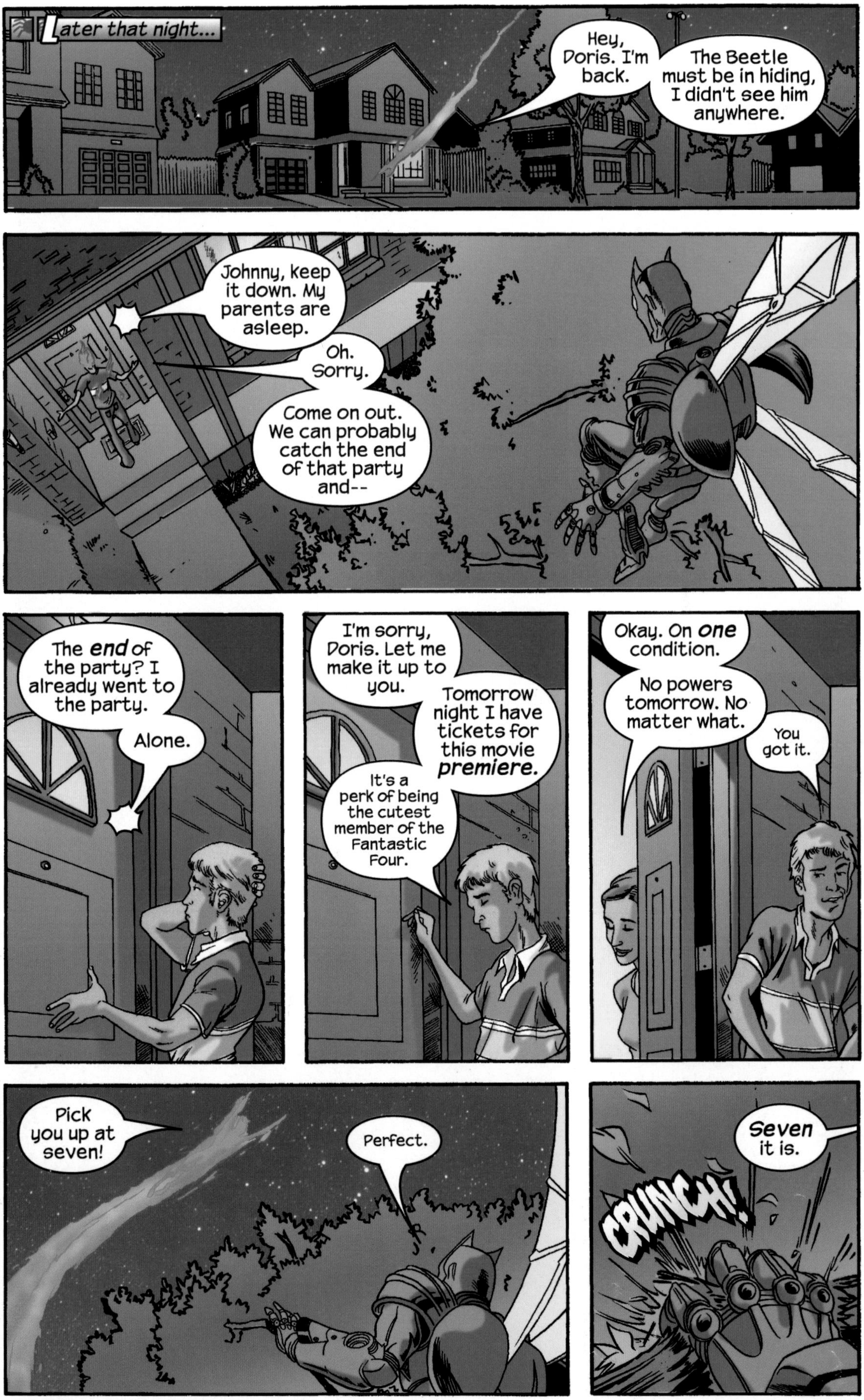
Later that night...
Hey, Doris. I'm back.
The Beetle must be in hiding, I didn't see him anywhere.
Johnny, keep it down. My parents are asleep.
Oh. Sorry.
Come on out. We can probably catch the end of that party and--
The *end* of the party? I already went to the party.
Alone.
I'm sorry, Doris. Let me make it up to you.
Tomorrow night I have tickets for this movie *premiere.*
It's a perk of being the cutest member of the Fantastic Four.
Okay. On *one* condition.
No powers tomorrow. No matter what.
You got it.
Pick you up at seven!
Perfect.
Seven it is.
CRUNCH!

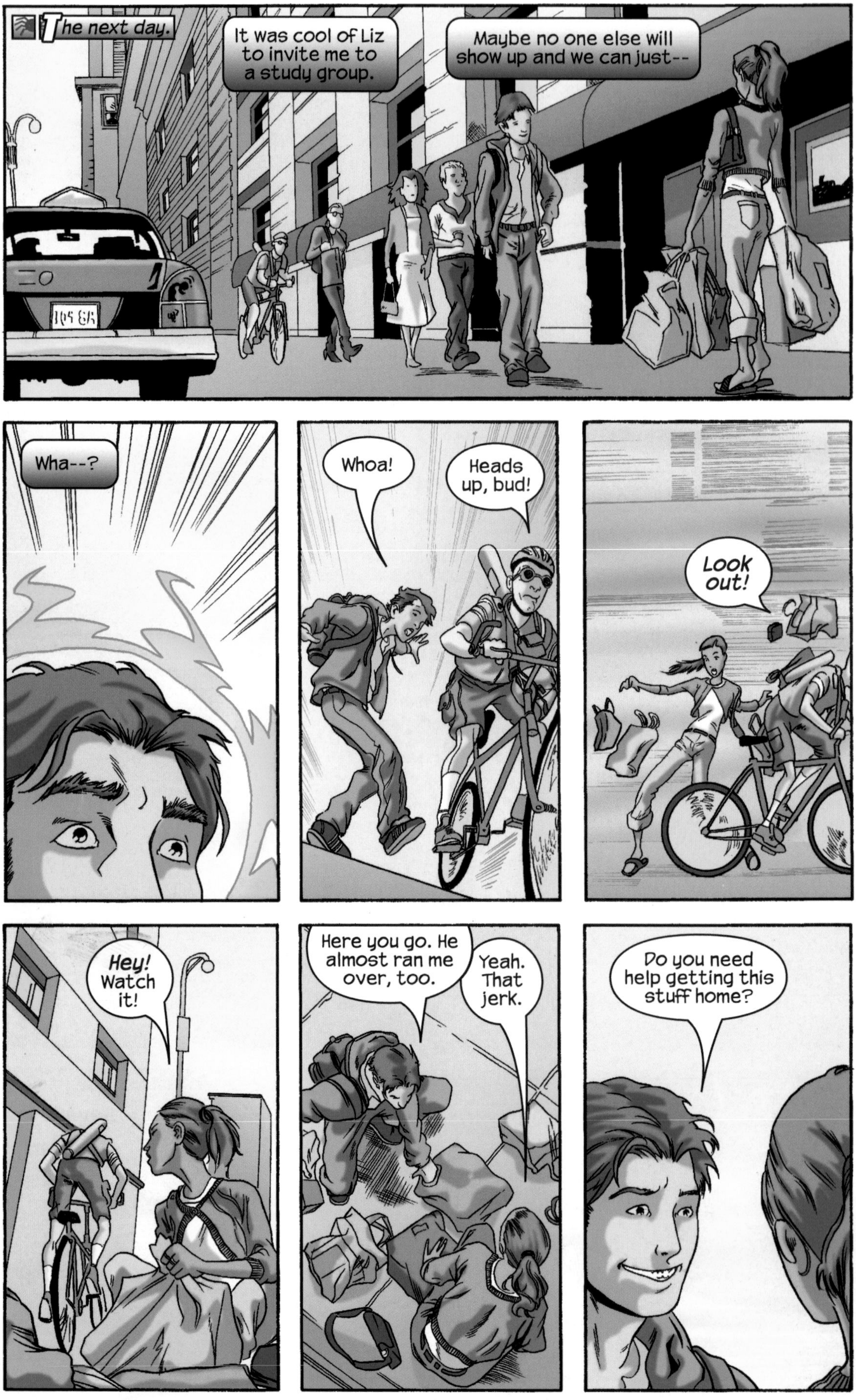
The next day.
It was cool of Liz to invite me to a study group.
Maybe no one else will show up and we can just--
Wha--?
Whoa!
Heads up, bud!
Look out!
Hey! Watch it!
Here you go. He almost ran me over, too.
Yeah. That jerk.
Do you need help getting this stuff home?

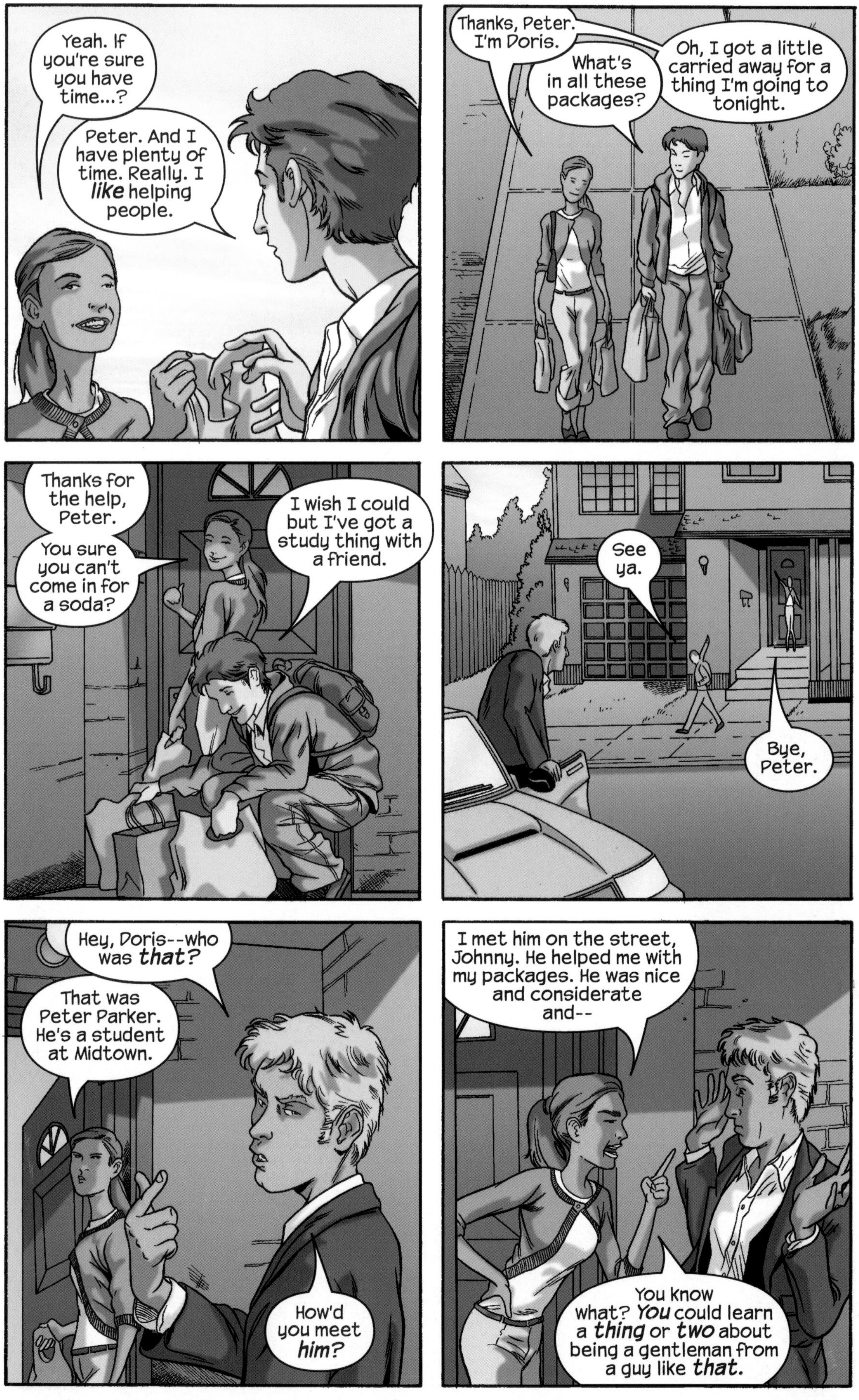
Yeah. If you're sure you have time...?
Peter. And I have plenty of time. Really. I *like* helping people.
Thanks, Peter. I'm Doris.
What's in all these packages?
Oh, I got a little carried away for a thing I'm going to tonight.
Thanks for the help, Peter.
You sure you can't come in for a soda?
I wish I could but I've got a study thing with a friend.
See ya.
Bye, Peter.
Hey, Doris--who was *that?*
That was Peter Parker. He's a student at Midtown.
How'd you meet *him?*
I met him on the street, Johnny. He helped me with my packages. He was nice and considerate and--
You know what? *You* could learn a *thing* or *two* about being a gentleman from a guy like *that.*

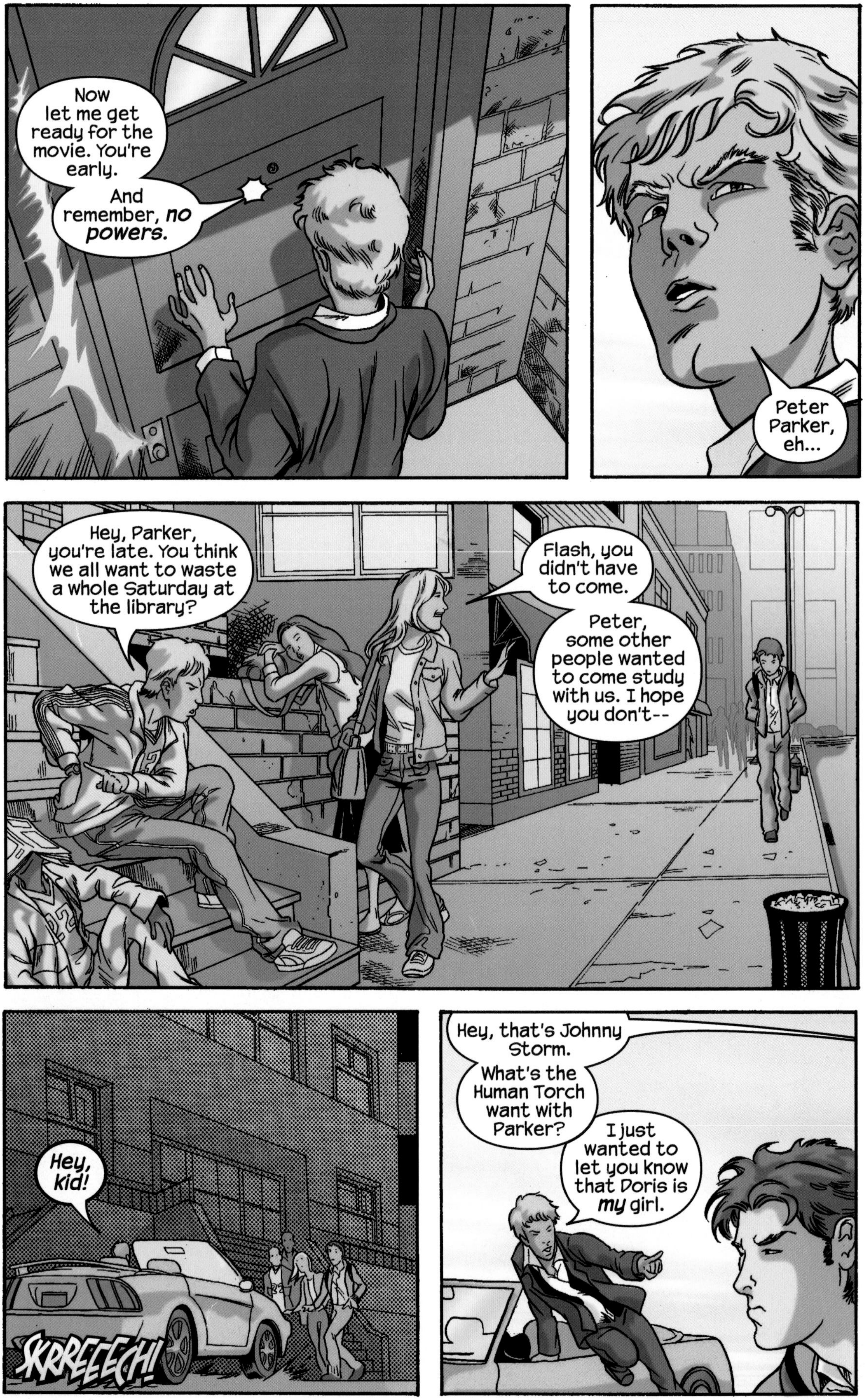
Now let me get ready for the movie. You're early.
And remember, *no powers.*
Peter Parker, eh...
Hey, Parker, you're late. You think we all want to waste a whole Saturday at the library?
Flash, you didn't have to come.
Peter, some other people wanted to come study with us. I hope you don't--
Hey, kid!
SKRREEECH!
Hey, that's Johnny Storm.
What's the Human Torch want with Parker?
I just wanted to let you know that Doris is *my* girl.

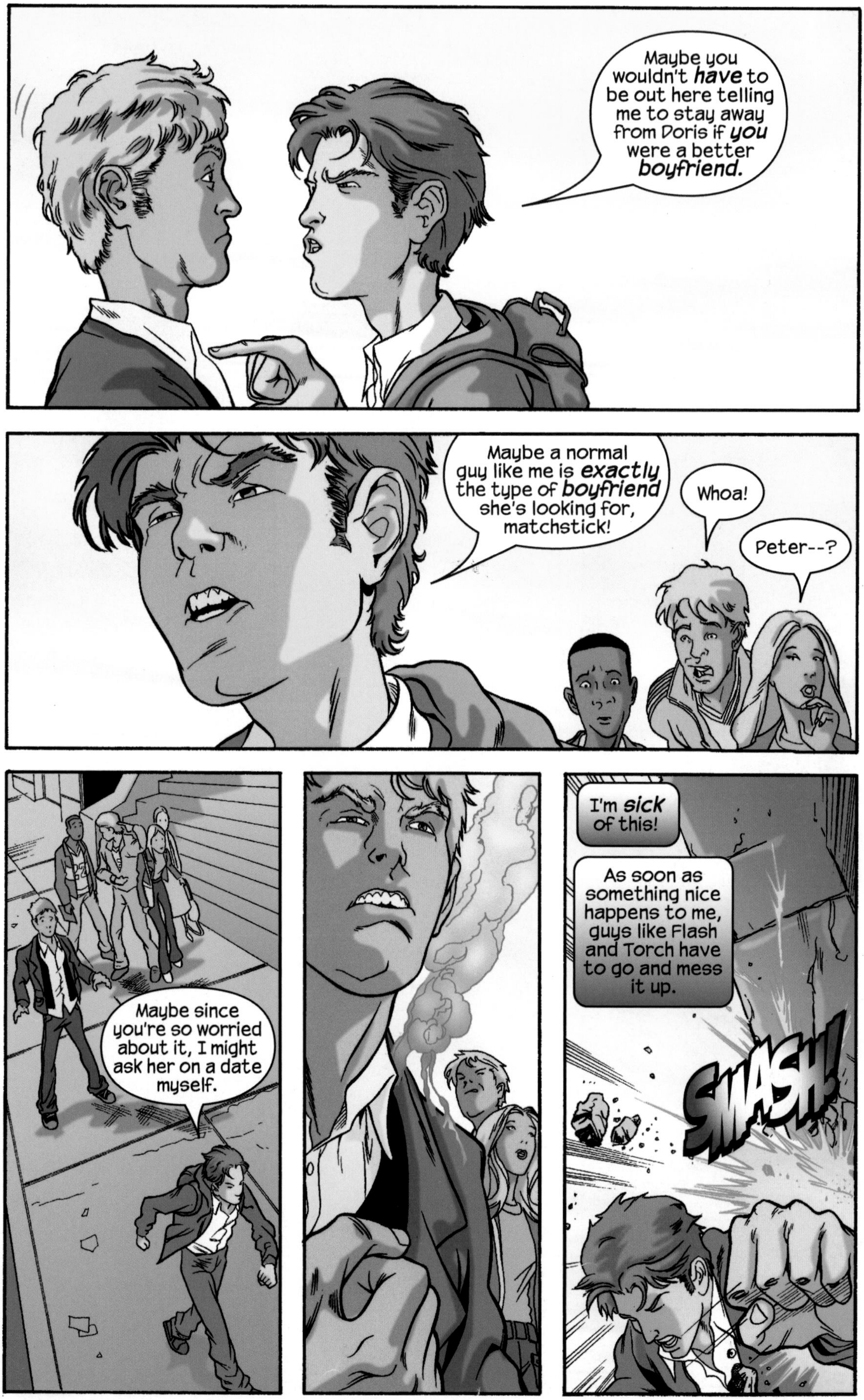
Maybe you wouldn't have to be out here telling me to stay away from Doris if you were a better boyfriend.
Maybe a normal guy like me is exactly the type of boyfriend she's looking for, matchstick!
Whoa!
Peter--?
Maybe since you're so worried about it, I might ask her on a date myself.
I'm sick of this!
As soon as something nice happens to me, guys like Flash and Torch have to go and mess it up.
SMASH!

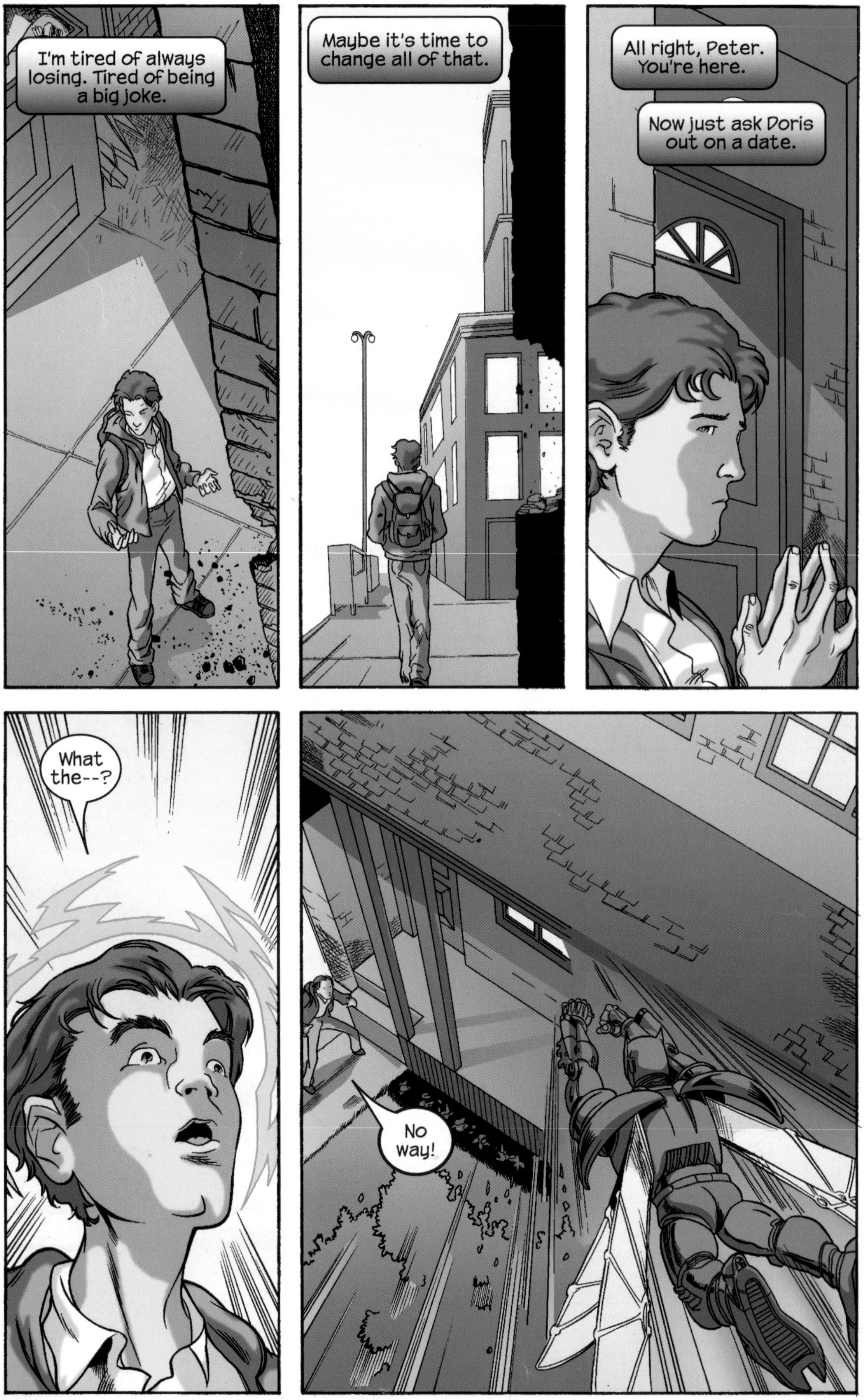
I'm tired of always losing. Tired of being a big joke.
Maybe it's time to change all of that.
All right, Peter. You're here.
Now just ask Doris out on a date.
What the--?
No way!

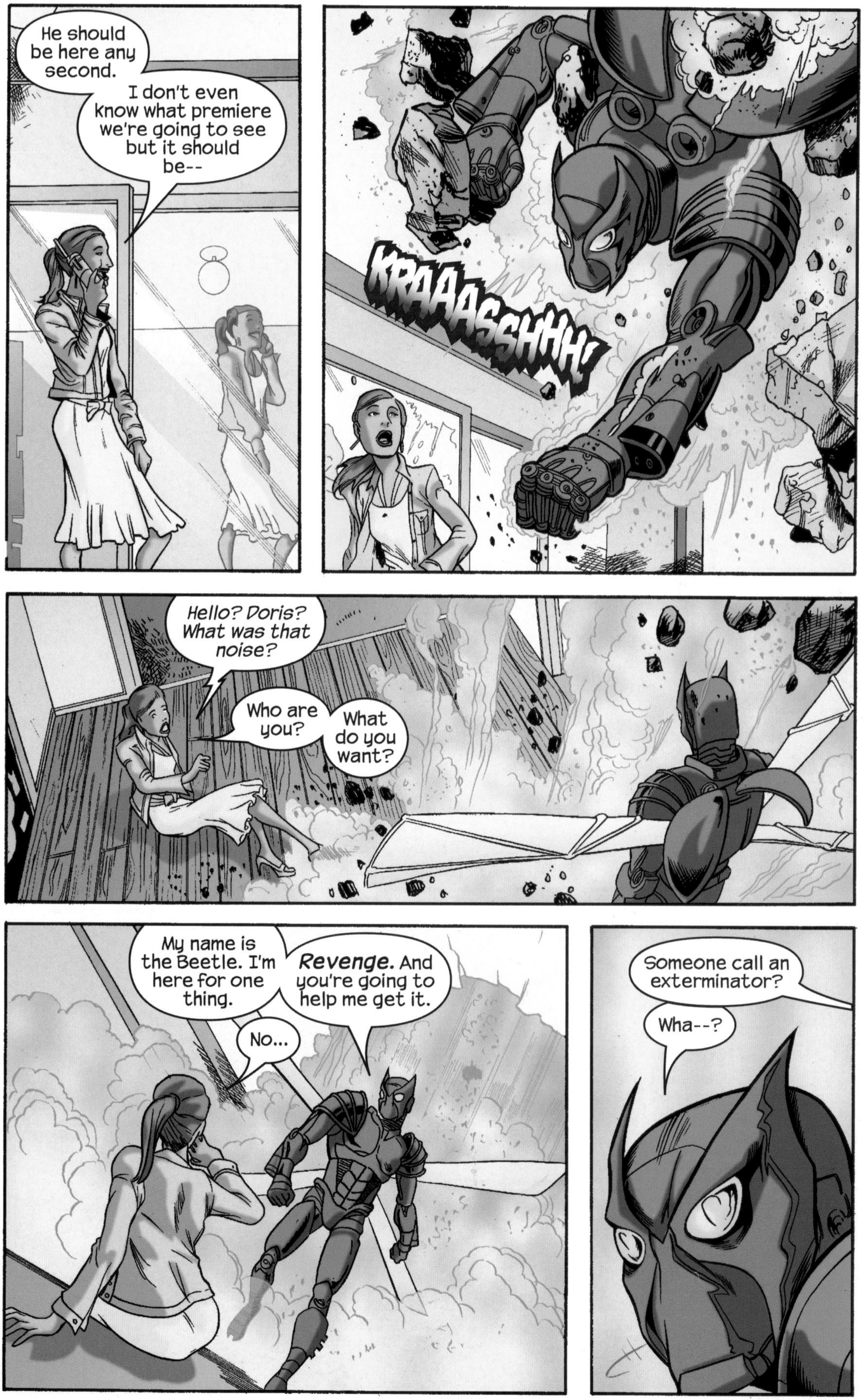
He should be here any second.
I don't even know what premiere we're going to see but it should be--
KRAAASSHHH!
Hello? Doris? What was that noise?
Who are you?
What do you want?
My name is the Beetle. I'm here for one thing.
Revenge. And you're going to help me get it.
No...
Someone call an exterminator?
Wha--?

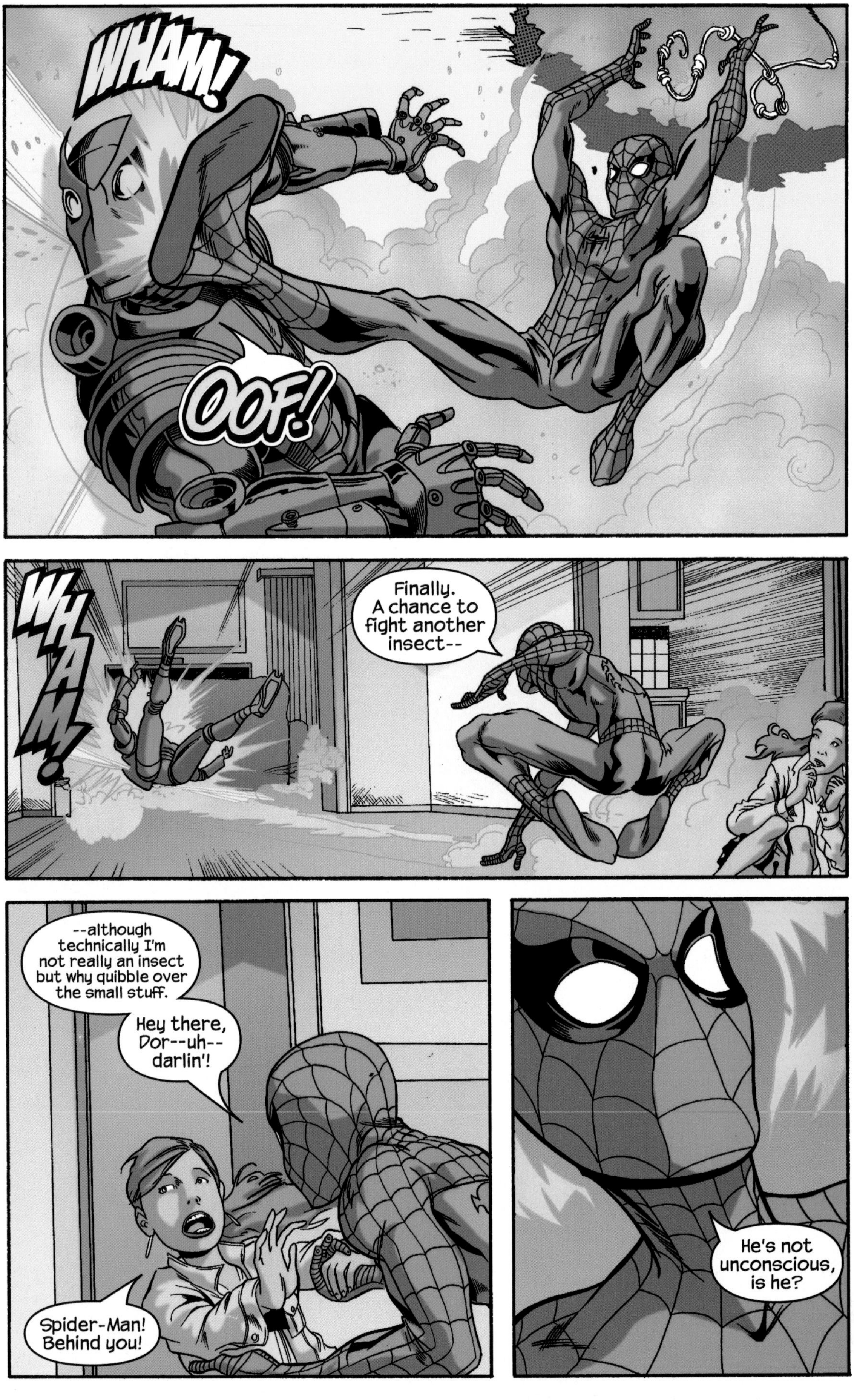
WHAM!
OOF!
WHAM!
Finally. A chance to fight another insect--
--although technically I'm not really an insect but why quibble over the small stuff.
Hey there, Dor--uh--darlin'!
Spider-Man! Behind you!
He's not unconscious, is he?

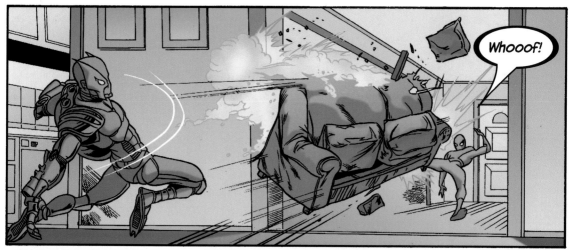

Whooof!

CRACK!

Let go of me!

This has *nothing* to do with you, Spider-Man!

Tell the Human Torch I have his girl and I'll be waiting for him at the docks.

Nice work, dope.

Letting a girl get kidnapped by the bad guy is not the best way to get a date.

Spidey?

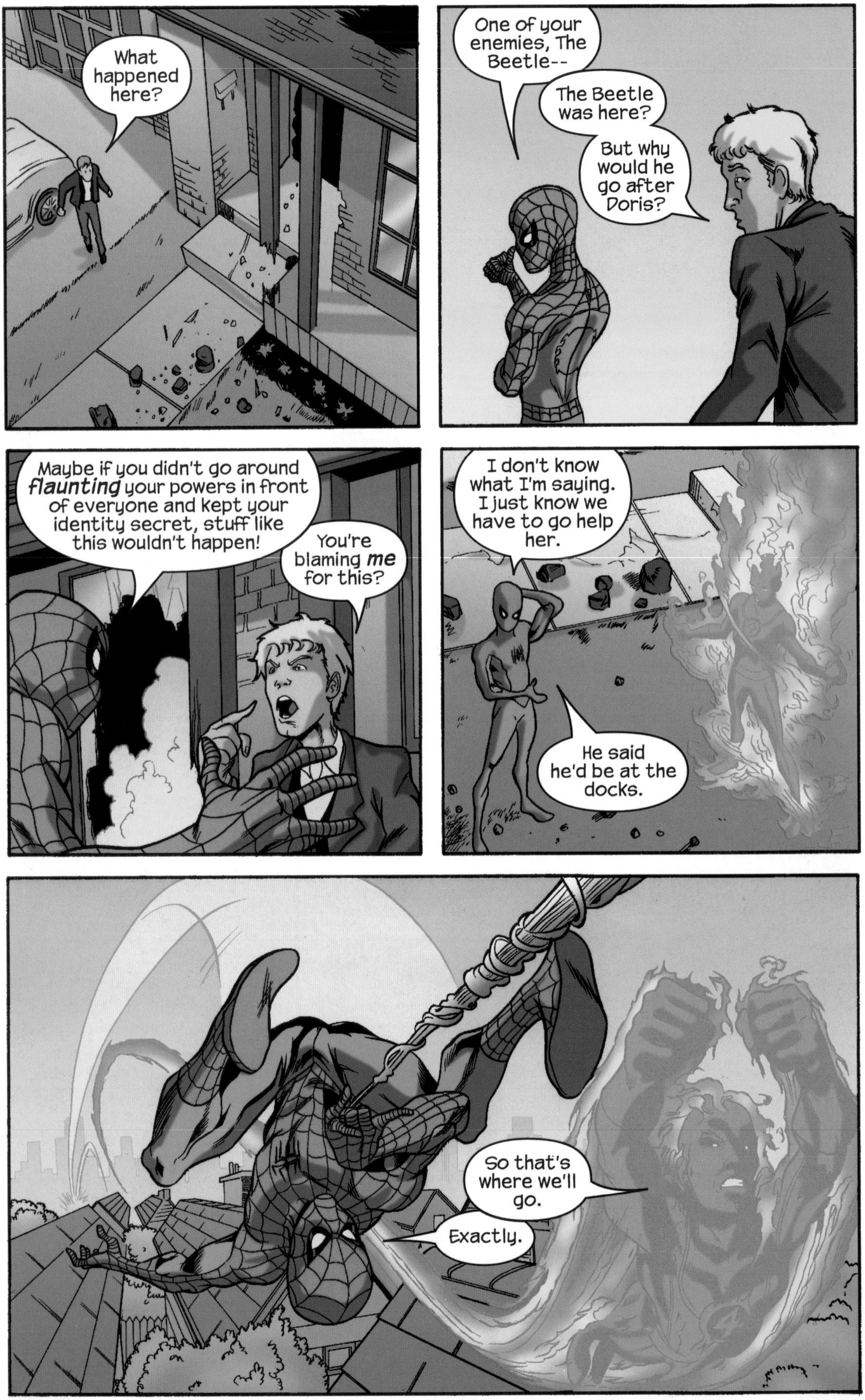
What happened here?
One of your enemies, The Beetle--
The Beetle was here?
But why would he go after Doris?
Maybe if you didn't go around *flaunting* your powers in front of everyone and kept your identity secret, stuff like this wouldn't happen!
You're blaming *me* for this?
I don't know what I'm saying. I just know we have to go help her.
He said he'd be at the docks.
So that's where we'll go.
Exactly.

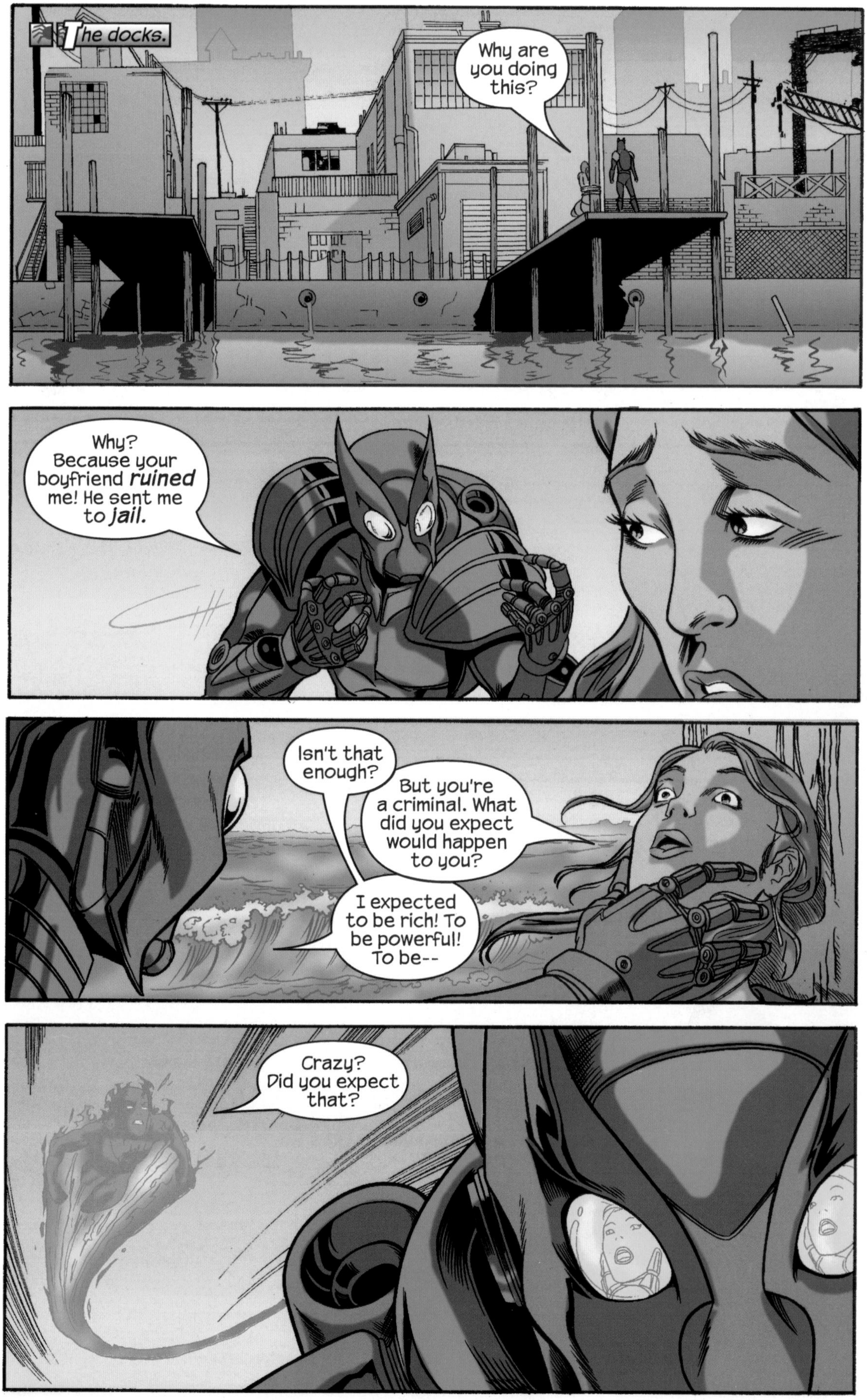
The docks.
Why are you doing this?
Why? Because your boyfriend ***ruined*** me! He sent me to ***jail.***
Isn't that enough?
But you're a criminal. What did you expect would happen to you?
I expected to be rich! To be powerful! To be--
Crazy? Did you expect that?

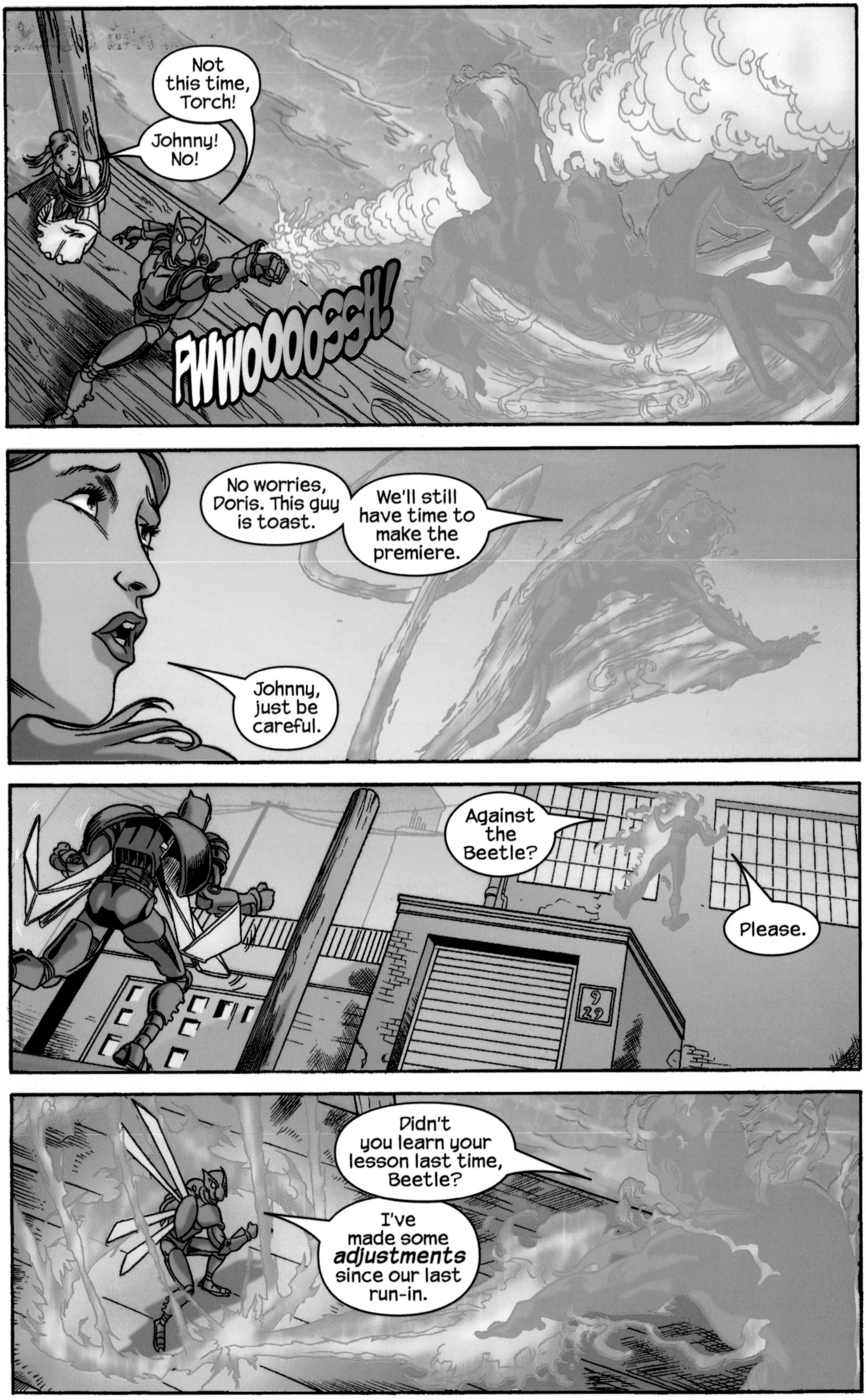
Not this time, Torch!
Johnny! No!
FWWOOOOSSH!
No worries, Doris. This guy is toast.
We'll still have time to make the premiere.
Johnny, just be careful.
Against the Beetle?
Please.
Didn't you learn your lesson last time, Beetle?
I've made some *adjustments* since our last run-in.

This time I'm *fireproof!*

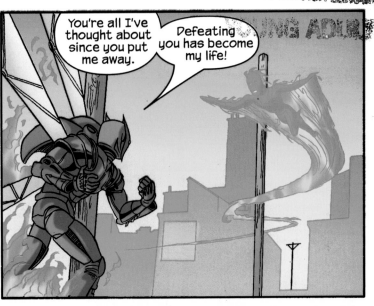

You're all I've thought about since you put me away.

Defeating you has become my life!

I'm flattered you feel so strongly about me, Beetle.

But, I have a girlfriend.

Always the jokester. Try to laugh this off.

Ahhh!

FWOOOSHH

Johnny!

Last time you caught me off guard. But this time I'm ready.

Why do you think I had you come to the *docks?*

I heard fire and water don't exactly mix.

SPLASH!

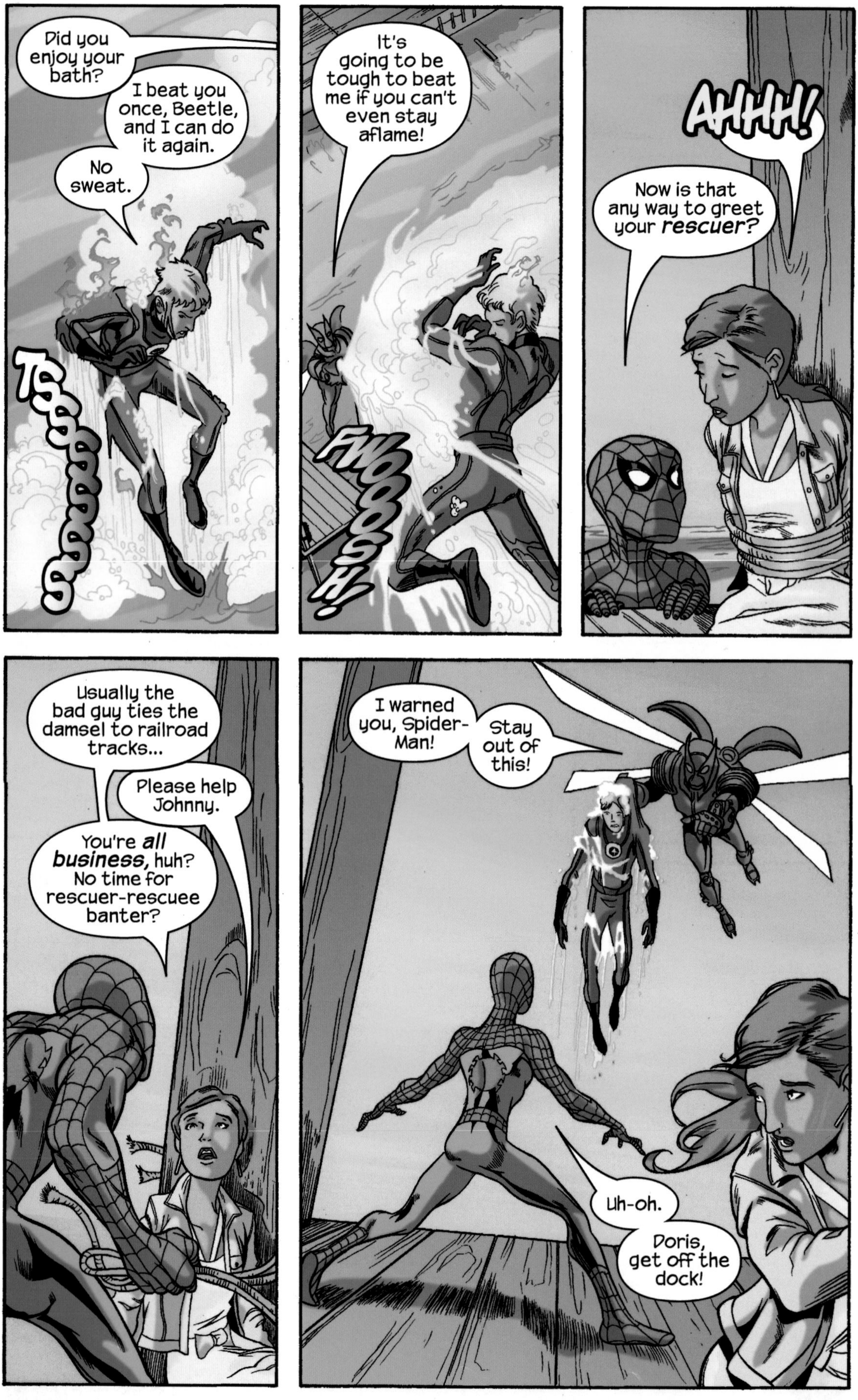
Did you enjoy your bath?
I beat you once, Beetle, and I can do it again.
No sweat.
TSSSSSSSSS
It's going to be tough to beat me if you can't even stay aflame!
FWOOOOSH!
AHHH!
Now is that any way to greet your *rescuer?*
Usually the bad guy ties the damsel to railroad tracks...
Please help Johnny.
You're *all business,* huh? No time for rescuer-rescuee banter?
I warned you, Spider-Man!
Stay out of this!
Uh-oh.
Doris, get off the dock!

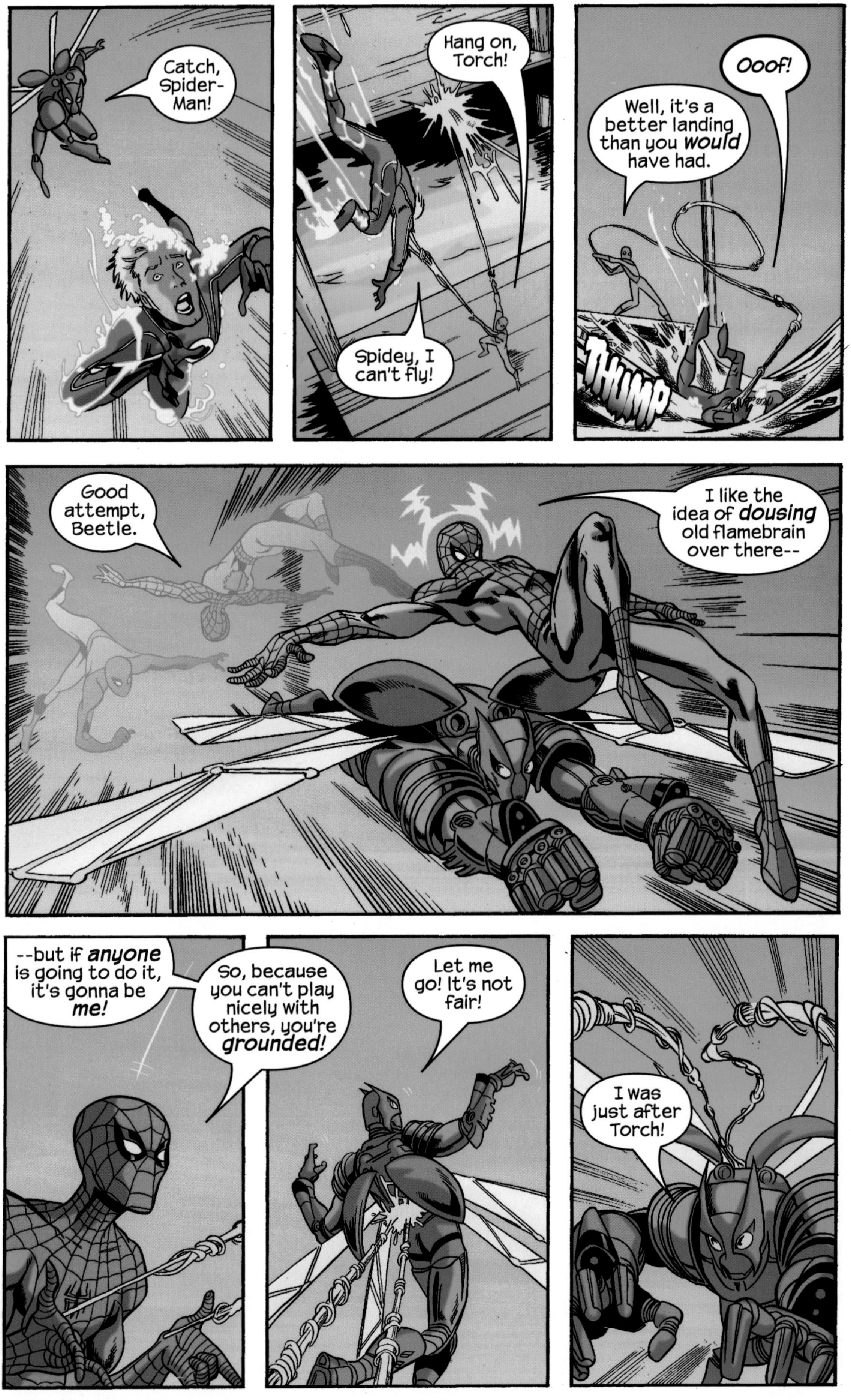

Catch, Spider-Man!
Hang on, Torch!
Spidey, I can't fly!
Ooof!
Well, it's a better landing than you *would* have had.
THUMP
Good attempt, Beetle.
I like the idea of *dousing* old flamebrain over there--
--but if *anyone* is going to do it, it's gonna be *me!*
So, because you can't play nicely with others, you're *grounded!*
Let me go! It's not fair!
I was just after Torch!

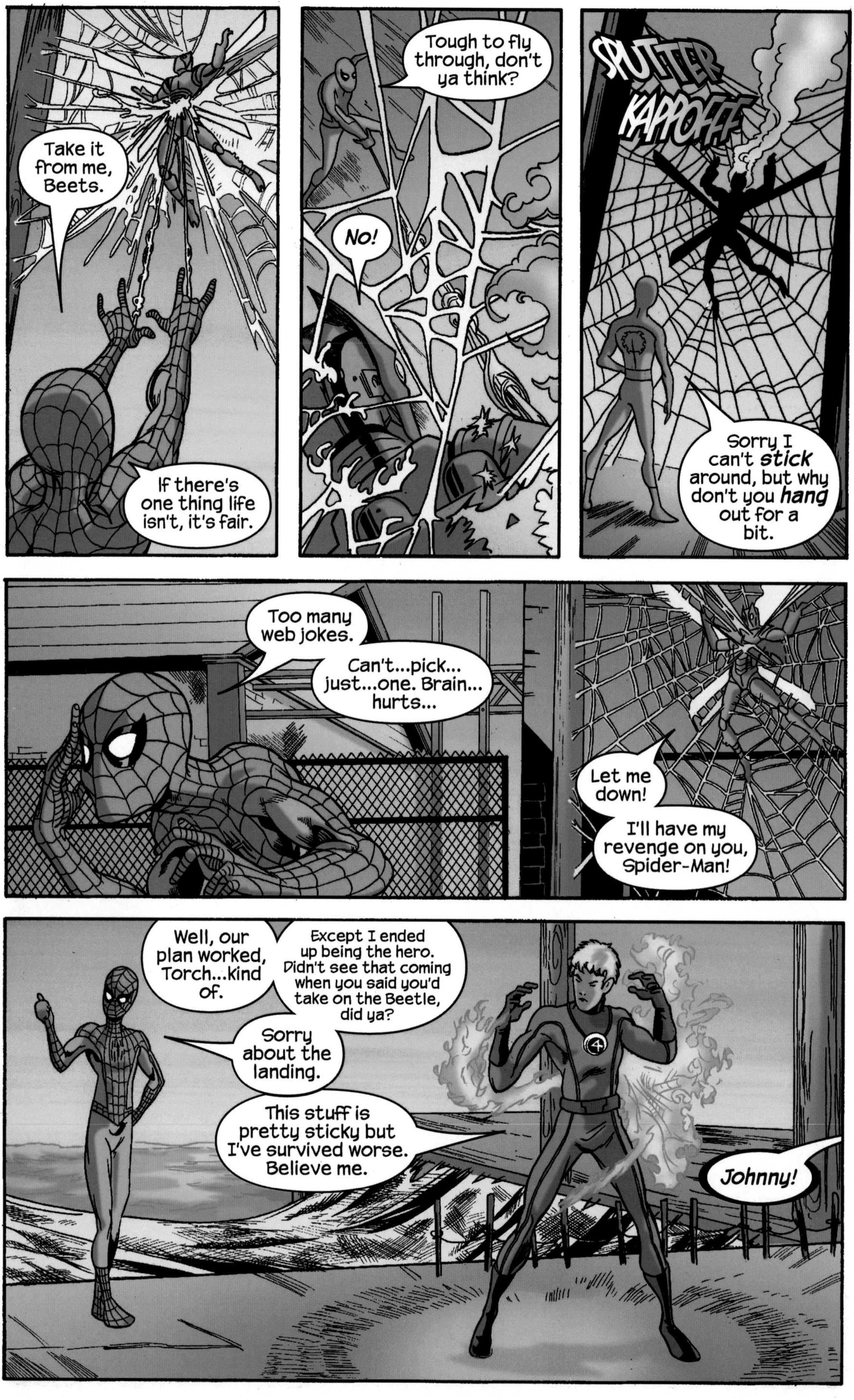
Take it from me, Beets.
If there's one thing life isn't, it's fair.
Tough to fly through, don't ya think?
No!
SPUTTER
KAPPOFFF
Sorry I can't stick around, but why don't you hang out for a bit.
Too many web jokes.
Can't...pick... just...one. Brain... hurts...
Let me down!
I'll have my revenge on you, Spider-Man!
Well, our plan worked, Torch...kind of.
Except I ended up being the hero. Didn't see that coming when you said you'd take on the Beetle, did ya?
Sorry about the landing.
This stuff is pretty sticky but I've survived worse. Believe me.
Johnny!

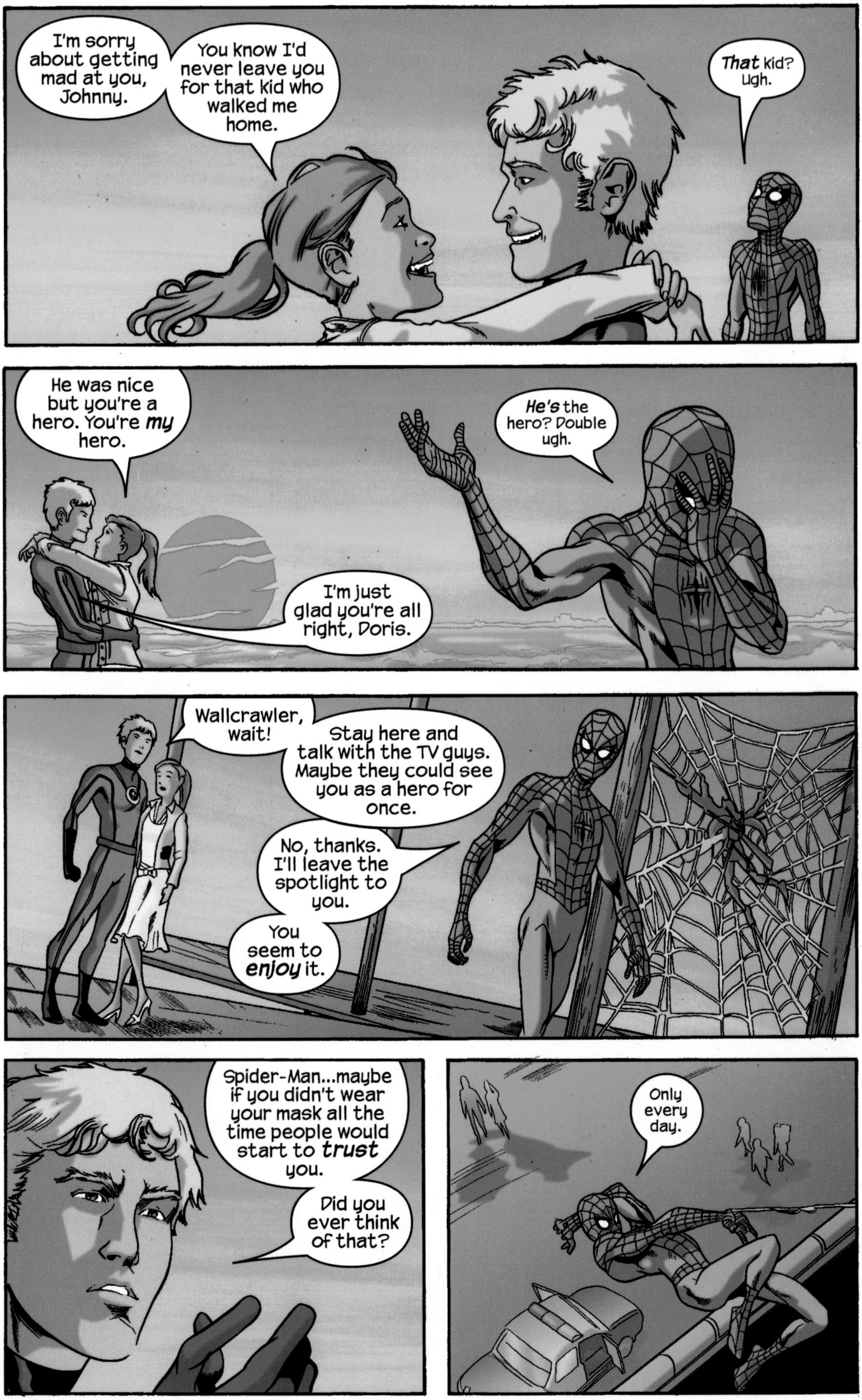
I'm sorry about getting mad at you, Johnny.
You know I'd never leave you for that kid who walked me home.
That kid? Ugh.
He was nice but you're a hero. You're my hero.
He's the hero? Double ugh.
I'm just glad you're all right, Doris.
Wallcrawler, wait!
Stay here and talk with the TV guys. Maybe they could see you as a hero for once.
No, thanks. I'll leave the spotlight to you.
You seem to enjoy it.
Spider-Man...maybe if you didn't wear your mask all the time people would start to trust you.
Did you ever think of that?
Only every day.

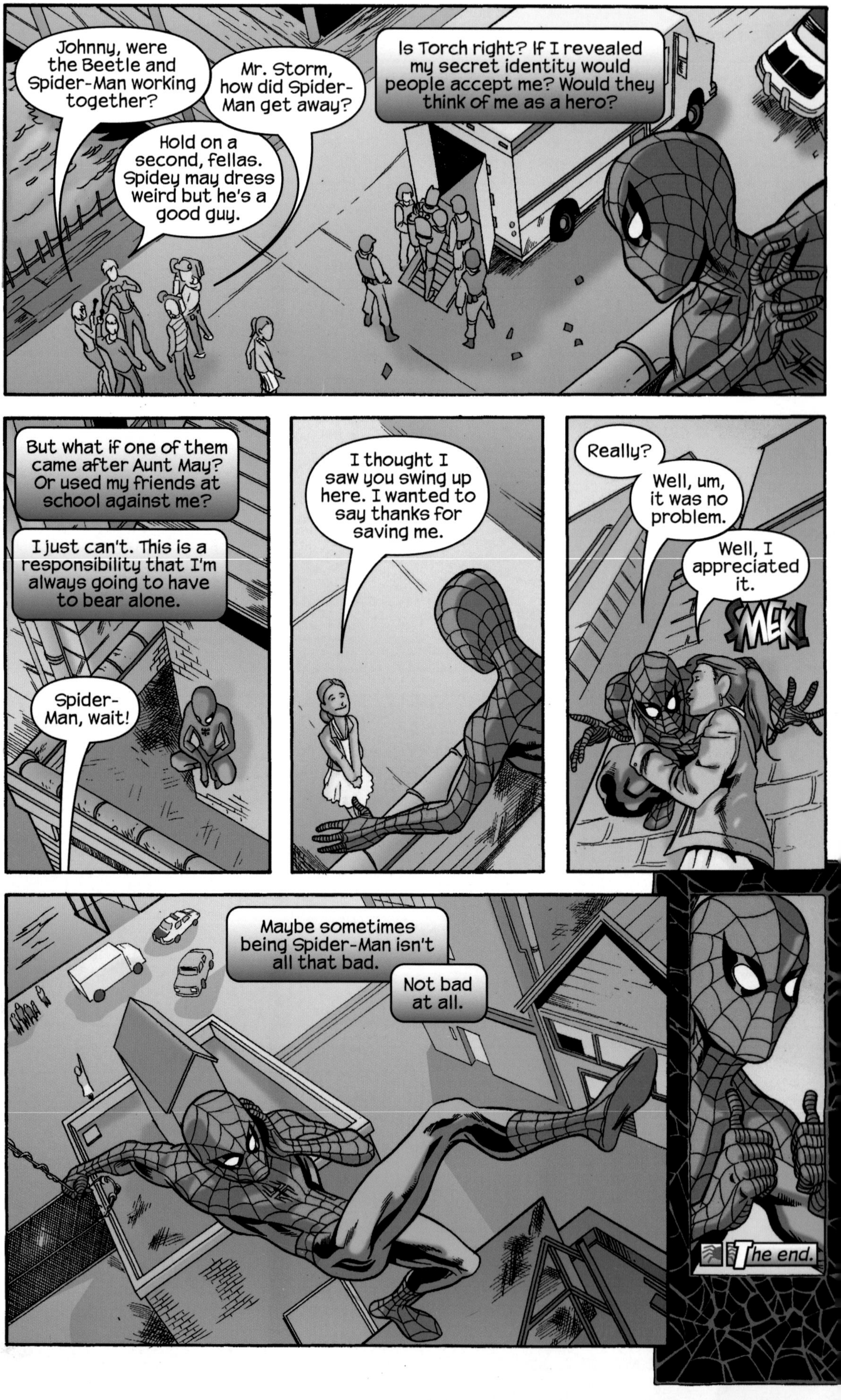
Johnny, were the Beetle and Spider-Man working together?
Mr. Storm, how did Spider-Man get away?
Hold on a second, fellas. Spidey may dress weird but he's a good guy.
Is Torch right? If I revealed my secret identity would people accept me? Would they think of me as a hero?
But what if one of them came after Aunt May? Or used my friends at school against me?
I just can't. This is a responsibility that I'm always going to have to bear alone.
Spider-Man, wait!
I thought I saw you swing up here. I wanted to say thanks for saving me.
Really?
Well, um, it was no problem.
Well, I appreciated it.
SMEK!
Maybe sometimes being Spider-Man isn't all that bad.
Not bad at all.
The end.